The Long Wait

by Annie Cobb
Illustrated by Liza Woodruff

The Kane Press
New York

Book Design/Art Direction: Roberta Pressel

Library of Congress Cataloging-in-Publication Data

Cobb, Annie.
    The long wait/by Annie Cobb; illustrated by Liza Woodruff.
        p.   cm. — (Math matters.)
    Summary: Two friends try to estimate how long they will have to wait in line to get on the fantastic new ride.
        ISBN 1-57565-094-0 (pbk. : alk. paper)
        [1. Approximation theory Fiction. 2. Amusement parks Fiction.]
        I. Woodruff, Liza, ill. II. Title. III. Series.
PZ7.C62975Lo 2000
[E]—dc21
                                                                    98-42682
                                                                         CIP
                                                                          AC

10 9 8 7 6 5 4 3 2 1

First published in the United States of America in 2000 by The Kane Press.
Printed in Hong Kong.

MATH MATTERS is a registered trademark of The Kane Press.

Josh and Zack were at Thrillenium Park.
The first thing they wanted to do was go
on the Cosmic Beetle. Their friends said
it was the most amazing ride *ever*.

Everybody else wanted to go on the
Cosmic Beetle, too. There was a long line.
Josh didn't want to wait. Zack did.

"This is going to take forever," said Josh.
"No it won't," said Zack. "We'll only have
to wait a few minutes."

Just then the line moved. Josh and
Zack were so busy arguing they didn't
notice. But the girl behind them did.

"See, it won't take long," said Zack.
The line stopped moving.
"See, I told you it would take forever,"
said Josh.

Zack had to admit the line did seem
to go on and on.

"How many people do you think are
ahead of us?" he wondered.

"I don't know, but it's a lot," said Josh.
He made a wild guess. "Maybe hundreds."

"Let's figure it out," said Zack. "There are 10 people in our row and, uhhh, about 6 rows. So I estimate 60."

"I say hundreds, you say 60," said Josh. "I'll go count them." As he ran off, he called back, "Save my place!"

9

At the front of the line, Josh started counting. He counted 57.

But as he started back, he saw a guy with a yoyo—a guy he didn't remember. Maybe he missed him. Maybe he missed other people, too. He'd better check his count.

By the time he reached Zack, the line was moving again.

"What took you so long?" Zack asked.

"I counted twice," Josh said. "First I got 57. Then I got 62! So 60 was a good guess—lots closer than mine."

A scary buzzing sound filled the
air. They looked up at the Cosmic
Beetle. People were riding inside the
legs. The legs swooped up and down,
and spun around, at the same time.

"Cool!" said Josh.

"Cool!" said Zack.

"Let's estimate how many people are on the ride," said Zack.

"You first," said Josh. This time Josh was going to think about his guess.

"Let's see," said Zack. "There are 6 legs—
and 2 people can ride in each leg. 2 times 6
is 12, so I say 12 people."

"But maybe some of the legs have only one
person. So I guess the number is between 6
and 12. I say 9," said Josh.

"I'll go count!" he told Zack. "Save my place!"

Josh went over to the exit gate. He watched the people get off the ride. They seemed very excited. "Awesome!" someone said. "My heart is still pounding," said someone else.

Josh counted everyone as they came out.
"8...9...10. I was close," Josh said to himself.
He had guessed 9.

The line still looked long when Josh got back. "We've been here forever," he complained.

"I'm the one who's been here forever," said Zack. "You've only stood in line for a few minutes."

"How much longer do you think it will be?" asked Josh.

"Let's time the ride," said Zack. "Then we can figure it out."

There was a burst of exploding lights. The Cosmic Beetle was coming down. Josh looked at his watch. The time was 1:20.

The next time the lights exploded, Josh looked at his watch again. The time was 1:25.

"The ride takes about 5 minutes," he said.

Josh peered at the line. "It looks like
there are about 40 people ahead of us now."

"And if 10 people go on each time," Zack
said, "that's 4 rides."

"The ride takes 5 minutes," said Josh.

"So we'll have to wait about 20 minutes,"
Zack guessed.

"Then I have time to get sodas!" Josh
said. "Save my place!"
When Josh got back, he couldn't see Zack.
"Over here," Zack called.

"Great! We're getting near the front of the line," said Josh. He could almost picture himself on the Cosmic Beetle. "How high do you think it goes?" he asked.

"Hmmm," said Zack. "It looks about as high as 3 Supersonic Slides, stacked one on top of the other."

"Wow!" Josh said. "I bet you can see the whole park from up there!"

SUPERSONIC SLIDE
HAVE THE RIDE OF YOUR LIFE
40 FEET TALL

Just then the line moved. Now there
were only 8 people ahead of them.

"We're next, Josh!" said Zack. "Josh?"

The girl behind Zack tapped his shoulder.
"Your friend said to save his place," she
told him.

Josh had run off again! It was almost their turn. Suppose he didn't make it in time? They would probably have to go back to the end of the line.

Where was Josh?

Josh was talking to Robotman—his favorite superhero—and getting his autograph.

There was a burst of exploding lights. The Cosmic Beetle was coming down. And still no Josh! After all that waiting! This couldn't be happening. It was a nightmare.

"JOSH!" yelled Zack as the gate was opened. "J-O-S-H!"

Up popped Josh. He was waving two napkins signed by Robotman.

"Look! he yelled. I've got Robotman's autograph!"

"You were with Robotman?" said Zack. "Cool!"

"Go!" said the girl behind them. "What are you waiting for?"

"Nothing!" Josh and Zack shouted at the same time.

They rushed through the gate.

Josh and Zack were spinning high above Thrillenium Park. Was it worth the long wait?
You bet it was!

Estimation Chart

Here are some ways you can estimate to find an answer.

1. About how tall is the tree?

   Hmmm... about 3 boys tall.

   $5 + 5 + 5 = 15$

   The tree about feet tall

   5'

   (*Hint:* use what you already know.)

2. There are about 10 people in each row. There are about 6 rows. About how many people in all?

   About 60 people

   10, 20, 30, 40, 50, 60

   (*Hint:* count by tens.)

3. Either 2 or 3 people can fit on a bench. There are 4 benches. About how many people can fit on the benches?

   $2 + 2 + 2 + 2 = 8$
   $3 + 3 + 3 + 3 = 12$

   Betw 8 and peop

   (*Hint:* use the least number and the greatest number.)

4. It takes about 9 minutes to bake a batch of cookies. About how long would it take to bake 4 batches?

   About 40 minutes.

   9 minutes is close to 10 minutes.
   $10 + 10 + 10 + 10 = 40$

   (*Hint:* use rounding.)

32